SUPERTATO

THE GREAT EGGSCAPE!

Meet Sue and Paul:

Sue Hendra and **Paul Linnet** have been making books together since 2009 when they came up with *Barry the Fish with Fingers*, and since then they haven't stopped. If you've ever wondered which one does the writing and which does the illustrating, wonder no more . . . they both do both!

For my mother, who taught me to hunt Easter eggs – P.L.

SIMON & SCHUSTER

First published in Great Britain in 2022 by Simon & Schuster UK Ltd • 1st Floor, 222 Gray's Inn Road, London, WC1X 8HB
Text and illustrations copyright © 2022 Sue Hendra and Paul Linnet
The right of Sue Hendra and Paul Linnet to be identified as the authors and illustrators of this work
has been asserted by them in accordance with the Copyright, Designs and Patents Act, 1988
A CIP catalogue record for this book is available from the British Library upon request
978-1-3985-1161-3 (PB) • 978-1-3985-1162-0 (eBook) • 978-1-3985-1231-3 (eAudio) • Printed in Italy • 10 9 8 7 6 5 4 3 2 1

SUPERTATO

THE GREAT EGGSCAPE!

SUE HENDRA
PAUL LINNET

SIMON & SCHUSTER
London New York Sydney Toronto New Delhi

It was night-time in the supermarket and all was quiet . . .

But The Evil Pea was up to something – it was all over his face.

"I love eating chocolate,

but not just ANY chocolate . . .

. . . ALL
OF THE
CHOCOLATE!
Mwah ha ha ha ha!"

Meanwhile, over in the seasonal aisle,
the veggies were in distress.
"Supertato, it's almost Easter and all
of the Easter eggs have gone!"
"Hmmm," said Supertato. "And I bet
I know *where* they've gone . . .

Pea! Where are you hiding?"

The pea was inside his Easter egg castle
and it was heavily guarded.
"Go away, Supertato," hissed the pea.
"The chocolate is mine, all mine!"

Supertato was livid. "You won't get away with
this, Pea!" And off he went to find the veggies.

"If we want our eggs back, we're going to need to get inside that castle – but how . . . ?"

Just then, Supertato caught sight of his reflection and an idea started to take shape.

"What are you going to do?" cried the veggies.

"Well," said Supertato, "with your help, we're going to give that pea . . .

.... a present!

First, I need you to collect up as much sparkly foil as you can find.

Next, cover me all over! That's right, veggies. Don't hold back!"

The veggies did as they were told and finally it was time for the finishing touch –

a big, fancy bow.

"EGGcellent!" mumbled Supertato from underneath the foil. "Now take me to that Pea! He won't be able to resist me."

The veggies rolled Supertato to the pea's fortress,

and presented their
rather dizzy gift.

"Oh, how sweet!" said the pea,
as the hench peas dragged it inside.

"You **really** shouldn't have . . .

. . . tried to trick me!" spat the pea in a rage.

"Yes, Supertato, looks like you've been FOILED AGAIN!
What do you think I am?
Some kind of NITWIT?!

A pretty egg like this needs to be tied up
with even MORE lovely ribbon,
don't you think?

And how about a special box to keep it all nice and fresh?

Now, where was I . . . ? Oh, yes, chocolate . . . I'm going to eat every single Easter egg in this whole supermarket and NO ONE is going to stop me. **Mwah ha ha ha ha!**"

The veggies could hear the commotion. "What are we going to do?" said Tomato. "Now we've got to save Supertato AND the Easter eggs. We're going to need a bigger plan . . ."

"I know!" said Carrot. "Let's make a giant animal that we can ALL hide inside! Then when the pea takes it into the castle, we'll jump out and save the day!"

"Wow!" said Tomato.
"What an original idea!

But what kind of animal . . . ?
Oooh, I know! A horse!"
"That's not very Easter-y,"
said Broccoli.

"I've got it!" said Cucumber,
grabbing a pencil.
"Let's make . . .

. . . an Easter chick!

The Evil Pea will
NEVER guess we're inside!"

So Tomato found something to use for the body.

Carrot spotted something to help make the nest,

and Cucumber searched out some sparkly foil to make it look like chocolate.

When they were finished, it looked fantastic,
but with the veggies inside it was very heavy indeed . . .
Somehow, Broccoli managed to carry it all the way to
the chocolate-y fortress and to Broccoli's delight . . .

"MORE chocolate? For me?" said The Evil Pea.

It looked as if the new plan was going really well . . .

. . . but it wasn't.
"You didn't think I was going to fall for that, did you?!
You veggies will never learn!" spat the pea.

"What an annoying collection
of Easter goodies!"

"We thought we'd save you, Supertato," whispered Carrot.

"It's the thought that counts," said Supertato, kindly.

"Well, it doesn't look as if the veggies are going to be having any Easter fun this year," said one pineapple to another.

And it was true. Things were looking bad – really bad. But just then, something very unexpected happened . . .

It used its
fluffy paws . . .

it used its
fluffy tail . . .

and it used a basket and
some springtime flowers.

With the greedy peas distracted,
Supertato and the veggies were able
to free themselves **and** the Easter eggs . . .

. . . and put them back in the seasonal aisle,
where they belonged!
"Thank you, Easter Bunny!" called the veggies,
but the bunny had gone.

"I don't feel well, Supertato," said The Evil Pea, looking quite a lot greener than usual. "That's because you've eaten too many Easter eggs, Pea. You've got exactly what you deserve."

"Do you think that was the REAL Easter Bunny?" asked Tomato.
"Well, I can't think who else it could have been," said Supertato. "Can you?"